A Trio of Tolerable Tales

A Trio of Tolerable Tales

Margaret Atwood

·

Illustrations by
Dušan Petričić

Groundwood Books
House of Anansi Press
Toronto   Berkeley

Collection published in Canada and the USA in 2017
by Groundwood Books
Second printing 2017

Groundwood Books / House of Anansi Press
groundwoodbooks.com

We acknowledge for their financial support of our publishing program the Canada
Council for the Arts, the Ontario Arts Council and the Government of Canada.

Canada Council
for the Arts

Conseil des Arts
du Canada

ONTARIO ARTS COUNCIL
CONSEIL DES ARTS DE L'ONTARIO
an Ontario government agency
un organisme du gouvernement de l'Ontario

With the participation of the Government of Canada
Avec la participation du gouvernement du Canada

Library and Archives Canada Cataloguing in Publication
Atwood, Margaret
[Short stories. Selections]
A trio of tolerable tales / Margaret Atwood ; illustrated by Dušan
Petričić.
Issued in print and electronic formats.
ISBN 978-1-55498-933-1 (hardback). — ISBN 978-1-55498-934-8 (epub).
— ISBN 978-1-55498-935-5 (mobi)
I. Petričić, Dušan, illustrator II. Atwood, Margaret. Rude
Ramsay and the roaring radishes. III. Atwood, Margaret. Bashful
Bob and Doleful Dorinda. IV. Atwood, Margaret. Wandering
Wenda and Widow Wallop's wunderground washery. V. Title.
VI. Title: Short stories. Selections.
PS8501.T86A6 2017   jC813'.54   C2016-905778-X
C2016-905779-8

Design by Michael Solomon

MIX
Paper from
responsible sources
FSC
www.fsc.org   FSC® C016245

CONTENTS

Rude Ramsay and the Roaring Radishes

For Madelaine and for R. and E. Cook,
who will eat almost anything.
M.A.

For my curious granddaughter Lara.
D.P.

Rude Ramsay resided in a ramshackle rectangular residence with a roof garden, a root
cellar and a revolving door. A rampart ranged
down the right-hand side of the run-down real
estate.

Residing with Rude Ramsay, who was red-
haired, were his revolting relatives, Ron, Rollo
and Ruby. They were rotund but robust, and
when not regaling themselves with rum, they
relaxed in their recliners, replaying reams of
retro rock 'n' roll records, relentlessly. This could
be rigorous.

While Ron read the racing results, Ruby
and Rollo regularly rustled up the repasts. They

roasted rice, raisins, rutabagas and rhinoceros. They rolled out reptiles with a rolling pin. They refrigerated rhubarb, and broiled ribs, raviolis and reindeer rinds on the rotisserie. The rice was rock-hard, the ribs rubbery, the raviolis wrinkled, the rhinoceros raw. The reptiles were still writhing, the rhubarb was runny, and the reindeer rinds were rotten.

Every Friday, Rude Ramsay rebelled.

"This repast is repulsive," he'd report. "The rice is riddled with roaches, the raisins are rancid, and the reindeer rinds reek. I feel like regurgitating!"

"Ramsay, you rash, repulsive, red-headed runt! How rude! Rinse your mouth out with rope!" raged Ramsay's revolting relatives, Ron, Rollo and Ruby. "Repent! Repent!"

"I refuse," retorted Ramsay.

Thoroughly riled, the three revolting relatives rose from the rejected repast and rushed after Ramsay, hurling ratchets, wrenches, wristwatches, rubber boots and radios, which rebounded off Ramsay's rear. But Ramsay was a

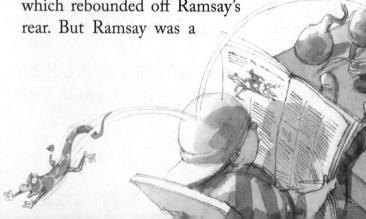

rapid runner, and he raced up to the roof garden and down to the root cellar and round and round the revolving door, until his robust but rotund relatives could no longer respire and required rest.

This ruckus was regarded by numerous raccoons, rabbits, robins, rollicking wrens and rowdy raggedy ravens, who were all roosting on

the right-hand rampart, relishing the race and repeating, "Rah! Rah!" raucously.

Ramsay's only friend was Ralph, the red-nosed rat, a rubicund rodent. While Ramsay reclined upon a rumpled rucksack near the trash heap, rubbing his rust-colored bruises, Ralph rummaged among the roach-riddled rice and the rancid raisins and the remnants of reeking rhinoceros, remarking, "Rubbish is ravishing to rats. We revel in rotten reindeer rinds."

"Ripping for you," Ramsay retorted wretchedly. "You are a rat. But I'm ravenous. All this repeated running round and round is ruining me. I refer also to the retch-making recipes I am required to devour, and which I resent. I am less robust than my revolting relatives. I am receiving a raw deal. It rankles!"

"You might rove to the other side of the rampart," reflected one of the raggedy ravens. "Relocate

your inner realm. Revive your rapport with nature! Refreshment awaits you there!"

"Be realistic," Ramsay replied. "The rampart is rough. It rises ridiculously high, and it is replete with rocks."

"I remember a round, Roman-vaulted rat hole," remarked Ralph the red-nosed rat, while grooming his greasy whiskers. "It traverses the rampart, and might be wriggled through."

"Risky," retorted Rude Ramsay. "If rammed in rather far and unable to retreat, I will repine. Then, if it rains, I will drown. Rigor mortis will set in, as well as wrinkles. I am reluctant."

"Rise to the occasion," responded Ralph. "Resist restrictions! Be rugged!"

Together the pair resolved to dare the Roman-vaulted but risky rat hole, which was crammed with rusty rivets, and assorted remnants, and the remains of rat nests, and was dripping with rivulets from the ragged

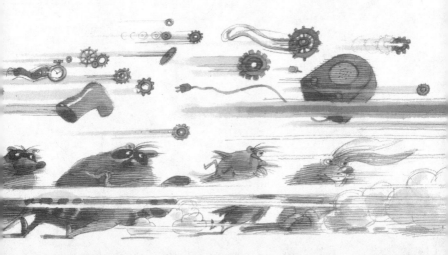

rents in the rodent-riddled rampart. Ralph rocketed recklessly through, but Ramsay had to crawl, creeping over dark rubble and through narrow turnings, ripping his trousers on sharp rocks, wrecking his rubber-soled runners and scraping his fingers. At last a rewarding ray of light pierced the remote end of the rat hole.

Ramsay emerged into a resplendent realm. A ranch-sized garden with a river rippling through it revealed itself to his regard, rendering Ramsay rhapsodic. A rowboat rocked restfully.

Roses enriched the redolent air with their aroma. Raspberry bushes were ranged in reassuring rows.

Ramsay roamed among the raspberry rows, ripping off ripe raspberries and cramming them into his mouth. Ralph rambled restlessly, ransacking the region for root vegetables.

"Radishes! Radishes!" Ralph briskly reported.

"Right you are!" Ramsay responded. For there, around a corner, were rows and rows of round red radishes, ready to be devoured. Surely they were organic! Ramsay hadn't relished a fresh radish ever since he could remember. What a rare treat!

Ramsay wrenched out a radish. He admired its roundness and redness. How crispy and crunchy it would be!

But the radish began roaring, "Robbers! Robbers! Replace that radish!"

Ramsay recoiled. "This is a roaring radish," he remonstrated. "It isn't even ripe. And it may have rabies — it bit me!"

Now all the radishes had ranged

themselves around Ramsay, rotating rambunctiously. The region resounded with their roars.

"Rotten luck," remarked Ralph, wrestling with a rabid radish. His whiskers were quivering with fear. "We must retreat!"

Together they ran towards the Roman-vaulted rat hole. The radishes were rolling towards them, roaring like organs.

But then a small girl appeared. She had a red ruffled frock, raven ringlets with ribbons and ribbed leg wear. Over her arm she carried a receptacle for roses and raspberries.

"Why are you robbing me of my radishes?" she queried.

"What radishes?" replied Ramsay reticently. The radishes had now stopped roaring and were resolutely re-rooting themselves in the ravaged radish rows.

"My name is Rillah," the small girl responded. "And you must be Rude Ramsay."

"You recognize me?" Ramsay was surprised.

"Only by remote reputation. I frequently hear your revolting relatives repeating that refrain. 'Rude Ramsay, you rash, repulsive, red-headed runt,' they rant. Would you like a rusk?" And she offered an assortment of rusks from her receptacle.

Ramsay and Ralph each reached for a rusk.

"Where do you reside?" Ralph inquired.

"In that romantic but recently restored rectory with the rotunda," replied Rillah.

Ramsay regarded the rectory. It was indeed romantic. Rhododendrons wreathed around it, fretwork trellises replete with trailing arbutus adorned it, a radiant rainbow arched above it.

"You must be royally rich," Ramsay remarked ruefully, remembering his own ramshackle residence. His trousers were ripped and his rubber-soled runners were wrecked. He resembled a ragamuffin. Surely Rillah would find him repellent. She would never be his friend. He wished she were a rat.

"Until recently I was rolling in rupees, but

they have become rather scarce. My situation," reflected Rillah, "is the reverse of yours. You are rude, but at least you have relatives, however revolting. I am refined, but my relatives, although outwardly respectable and refulgently attired, are lacking in rectitude.

"They rented a veritable regatta of Rolls Royces, but they fell into arrears on revenues. When the rent collector arrived, they all ran off, some by the road, some by rail, revealing no remorse. I have been rejected. No one has rescued me. Also, I am bored." And she released a tear.

"Cheer up," said Ramsay robustly. "Do not repine. Let's explore the rectory!"

Ramsay, Rillah and Ralph the red-nosed rat rambled all over the recently restored but romantic rectory. They reviewed the rotunda, which had a wide range of purloined reading materials, and the gallery filled with fraudulent rococo artworks, forged by professionals, and the cellar with racks and racks of rare beverages ruthlessly plundered by Rillah's rascally relatives. At last they reached the rumpus room.

"This is the rumpus room," remarked Rillah regretfully, "but there has never been a rumpus in it. My relatives, though racketeers, were too

refined for rumpuses. How I would relish regarding a real rumpus!"

"Your request is my resolve," replied Ramsay with a respectful gesture. "Return with me!"

So Ramsay, Rillah and Ralph the red-nosed rat wriggled back through the Roman-vaulted rat hole and reached the rectangular residence, where Ramsay's revolting relatives, Ron, Rollo and Ruby, replete with rum, were relaxing in their recliners to the resounding rhythms of rock 'n' roll.

"Ready?" inquired Ramsay.

Rillah grinned in a refined but riotous manner.

"Rotten reindeer rinds reek, and so do Ron, Rollo and Ruby!" Ramsay blared. "And your rock 'n' roll records are ridiculous!"

"Ramsay, you rabble-rouser! You are outrageous!" Ron, Rollo and Ruby rose from their recliners like red-eyed rattlesnakes and went on the rampage. What a ruckus! Ramsay raced up to the roof garden, reversed direction, reeled through the root cellar, then round and round the revolving door, while his revolting relatives hurled ratchets, wrenches, wristwatches, radios and rubber boots at his rear. But this time Ramsay ran so rapidly that they missed.

At last the revolting relatives ran out of steam and relapsed into a recumbent posture.

"Oh, Ramsay! That was a real rumpus!" trilled

Rillah. "You may be rude, but you can run with a rapidity that erases boredom!"

"I would be less rude if I resided in the romantic rectory, surrounded by rhododendrons," replied Ramsay, "and could eat raspberries and rusks, instead of raw rhinoceros and rancid raisins."

"True," Rillah responded. "And I would be less tearful. To acquire a friend is refreshing, as well as reassuring."

"Do you like rats?" Ramsay queried, for it had occurred to him that the arrival of a new friend might cause Ralph to feel repudiated.

"There are few creatures I adore more than a rubicund, red-nosed rodent," Rillah replied, stroking Ralph's fur with terms of endearment. "Also, he will crunch up any roaches that may stray from the run-down side of the rampart."

"What about the rabid roaring radishes?" inquired Ramsay.

"They regard me as a robber and will relentlessly rend me to shreds."

"They are not real radishes," replied Rillah. "They are robot replicas, cleverly arranged to repel intruders. I will re-program them so they will be neutral in regard to you."

So, while the raccoons, rabbits, robins, wrens and raggedy ravens all roosting on the rampart cheered, Ramsay, Rillah and Ralph the red-nosed rat crawled back through the Roman-vaulted rat hole …

… and romped rapturously among the roses, beside the rippling river, under the radiant rainbow.

BASHFUL BOB

and

DOLEFUL DORINDA

For Rowan.
M.A.

To Rastko, my grandson.
D.P.

When Bob was a baby, he was abandoned in a basket, beside a beauty parlor. His bubble-headed mum, a brunette, had become a blonde in the beauty parlor, and was so blinded by her burnished brilliance that baby Bob was blotted from her brain. By and by she became dismayed and bought an advertisement — "Baby in basket. Does not have a bat-shaped birthmark" — but it drew a blank.

Bob boo-hooed until he was blue from bonnet to bottom, but nobody came.

Luckily, beside the beauty parlor there was a vacant block, bestrewn with bushes, buttercups and benches. It was beloved of dogs, who would bounce balls and bury bones there. A boxer, a beagle and a borzoi heard Bob's bawling.

"Is it a buppy?" said the boxer, who talked through his nose.

"No, it's a biped," replied the beagle. "It must be a bird!"

"Not a bird, a baby! What bad behavior, to abandon it!" barked the borzoi. "We must be benevolent!"

The boxer, the beagle and the borzoi bounded into boutiques and burgled bundle buggies. They brought baby Bob bottles, booties and blankets. When Bob became bigger, they brought bananas, blueberries, baked beans, beets and broccoli. The broccoli made Bob burp.

The dogs were Bob's best buddies. They besieged bargain basements and brought Bob balloons, basketballs, blue jeans and boxes of building blocks. They also brought bundles of

buttered bread, barrelsful of bran flakes, and bunches and bunches of blackberries. Bombarded with abundant edible boodle, Bob became even bigger. Soon he was no longer a baby, but a boy.

But Bob was bashful. He did not believe he was a boy, and barked when bothered. He was bewildered by blithering barbers, blathering butchers, bun-bearing bakers and belligerent bus drivers, and would bound behind bushes or burrow under benches when they blundered by. He would bite busy businessmen in their briefcases.

"Bob is a boy," said the borzoi. "He does not belong with dogs."

"It is not broper," said the boxer.

"What will become of him?" said the beagle.

Bob's dog buddies were bemused.

On a block beside Bob, lived Doleful Dorinda. Dorinda's dad and darling mother had disappeared in a dreadful disaster when she was still in diapers, and she had been dumped on distant relatives.

Dorinda was adorable, with dozens of dimples and a disarming charm. But although the distant relatives were dripping with diamonds and had a desirable address, they behaved despicably. They dispensed not a dollar on Dorinda; they didn't dole out a dime.

"Dorinda is a dope," they declared. "She is a dimwit. She is a drag. She is a dumb downer. Doleful Dorinda!"

They dressed Dorinda in dust mops and dingy dungarees. They made her doze on a dank and dubious duvet in a derelict dumpster, beside a deep drain full of deadly diseases, such as diphtheria. She had to drudge from dawn to dusk, dabbing with a dust mop and dealing with dirty dishes in a disreputable dive, where dirty-deed-doers drank daiquiris. She had nothing to devour but defunct underdone ducks, dangerously deep-fried day-old hot dogs, stale-dated doughnuts and deplorable dairy products, deficient in Vitamin D and also disgusting. It was dire.

Dorinda became depressed. "Drat these darned dirty dishes," she declaimed. "I detest my distant relatives! I desire to be dealt with decently! I do not deserve such a dismal deal!"

One dark drizzly December day, Dorinda departed. She packed some doughnuts and deplorable dairy products and several extra dust mops into a discarded duffel bag.

"I defy doubt!" she declared. "Destiny, however distressing, will not defeat me! I disdain despair!"

Drenched by a downpour, dragging her duffel bag and dreadfully bedraggled, Doleful Dorinda was trudging doggedly across Bashful Bob's vacant block when she heard a bark. Two bright but blinking eyes were beaming from behind a bush. Dorinda bent back a branch. It was not a dog, but a bashful boy!

"I am no desperado," said Dorinda.

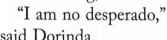

"May I share your domicile?" This was daring, as a barking boy might bite, but Dorinda was so damp she did not give a dastardly darn.

"Bow-wow," barked Bob.

Dorinda decided to dedicate herself to teaching Bob to talk. The boxer, the beagle and the borzoi were delighted! They burst into a bookstore and brought Dorinda and Bob a dictionary. Day by day Dorinda and Bob delved into it. Though sometimes discouraged, Bob soon went from bite-sized

words like "did" and "dot" and "bat" and "but" to difficult ones like "dirigible" and "ballistic."

"Bob is making brogress!" barked the boxer.

Bob beamed.

One day a bewildered buffalo bounded over a barrier at a nearby botanical garden. It had been placed there by a befuddled and bungling bureaucrat, who had botched its diploma and declared it to be a big begonia.

"Beware! Beware! A dangerous beast!" bleated all the barbers, bakers, butchers and bus drivers for blocks around, as they blundered in every direction.

The buffalo raised billows of dust. It dismembered daisies; it demolished daffodils and day care centers. Horns beeped and blared. Businessmen blustered. Babies blubbered.

"Bob! Bob! We must do something!" beseeched Dorinda.

"Buffalos bother me," said Bob. "They butt you in the behind. Besides, all those barbers, bakers, butchers and bus drivers would behold me. That would make me bashful. I'd rather be in the burrow under the bench."

"No time for bashfulness," said Dorinda. "Duty beckons!"

Dorinda daringly distracted the buffalo by brandishing her dust mops and dancing like a dervish. Bob, too, behaved bravely. He deployed his dog buddies around the bewildered buffalo, and they all barked beautifully.

"Do not distrust us! We will not betray you!"

barked the boxer, the beagle and the borzoi. "You are not a big begonia, you are a buffalo! It was all a bureaucratic blunder!"

The buffalo, being bilingual, understood their barking and became benign. After devouring a bucketful of barley and a barrel of stale-dated doughnuts, it departed in a boxcar for Alberta where it belonged.

"You are no longer Bashful Bob," declared Dorinda. "You are Brave Bob!"

"And you are no longer Doleful Dorinda. You are Daring Dorinda," said Bob.

"We will get our bictures in the bapers," said the boxer.

And they did.

Then Dorinda's dad and darling mother, who had been digging their way out of the debris of the dreadful disaster for dozens and dozens of days, recognized their dear daughter Dorinda from her dimples.

Dorinda's distant relatives were dismayed by the disclosure of their abysmal behavior and departed in disgrace.

And Bob's bubble-headed mum, who was now a brunette again and had been deploring her distracted behavior at the beauty parlor, spotted Bob's biography in the paper.

"He was abandoned in a basket! And he does not have a bat-shaped birthmark! He must be my baby, Bob!" she blurted, and begged Bob's forgiveness. In addition, Bob's dad was gratified, as he had been distinctly disturbed by Bob's abrupt and baffling disappearance.

Together, all four parents bought a bungalow with abundant bedrooms, a dining room

in which dishes of delicacies could be devoured and a bounteous backyard, big enough for basketball and burying bones, with bunches of bushes behind which Bob could bound when feeling bothered as he still did sometimes.

And so Brave Bob and Daring Dorinda and their parents — not to mention Bob's dog buddies, the boxer, the beagle and the borzoi — dwelt in the bungalow in blinding bliss, delirious with delicious delight.

WANDERING WENDA

AND
WIDOW WALLOP'S
WUNDERGROUND
WASHERY

For Madelaine and Rowan.
M.A.

For my restless grandchildren.
D.P.

Wenda was a willowy child with wispy hair and wistful eyes. When she was just a wee one, her wise and watchful parents were whisked away by a weird whirlwind.

After that, Wenda had wandered here and wandered there, wearing a well-worn worsted sweater that was too wide for her, and wondering when she would find them.

"Where, oh where could they be?" she wailed.

One day, Wenda saw a WANTED poster. The words were

WANTED!
WIZARD WILLUP, WIELDER OF WHIRLWIND WAND!
FOR WHIPPING UP WEIRD WHIRLWINDS
WHOPPING REWARD!

"Well," said Wenda. "I wonder!"

When weak with hunger, Wenda waited beside a wagonette that sold withered-up wieners. Sooner or later there would be wodges of wiener in the wastebin, which Wenda would wolf down.

One week, Wenda heard a whimper. It came from a wild animal that was worryingly weak and wobbly.

"Could you spare a wodge of wiener," it whispered.

"Are you a wombat?" whispered Wenda, who had once seen a wombat in a waiting room.

"No way," whispered the animal. "I am a woodchuck!"

"But woodchucks eat wood!" whispered Wenda.

"What do you think is in those wieners?" whispered the wood-chuck.

So Wenda gave it a wodge of wiener.

"Wow!" whispered the woodchuck. "Could be worse!"

"You're welcome," whispered Wenda as they walked away together. They were whispering so the whiskery wiener-wagonette vendor wouldn't whack them for wolfing down wodges of withered-up wieners out of his wastebin.

"Why are you in a town, instead of in the woods?" asked Wenda.

"I once widened rabbit warrens," said the woodchuck, "and eavesdropped on wolves. I know wads of wolf watchwords! Then I wandered away, because I wanted to see the world. But the world has too many wheels, windows, waifs and strays, and wrong turnings."

"You are so warm and wuzzy," said Wenda, as the two wanderers waited out the wintry wind behind a pile of wastepaper. "I will call you Wesley."

"Wurr, wurr," purred the woodchuck, wrapped in half of Wenda's well-worn worsted sweater.

Next Wednesday Wenda and Wesley were wandering in a westerly direction when a wooden wagon with wide wheels drawn by two white worn-down Welsh ponies paused beside them. The words written on the wagon were

A woman with one wonky eye, a wrinkly nose with a wen, three warty chins and wiry eyebrows was staring at them. She was wearing a well-starched waistcoat, a waterproof, Wellington boots and a wimple made of wrapping paper, and was waving a wicked-looking whip.

"Why are you wandering among the wastebins in this wishy-washy witless way?" asked Widow Wallop.

"My wise and watchful parents were whisked away by a weird whirlwind," said Wenda. Under her well-worn worsted sweater, Wesley was growling a worrisome woodchuck growl.

"Then you are a waif and a stray! Come with Widow Wallop!" said the woman, whisking Wenda into the wagon before she even had time to say, "No way!"

Widow Wallop wadded Wenda into a wicker basket and whipped the worn-down white Welsh ponies until they whizzed ahead, whinnying weakly.

"Wait! Wait!" wailed Wenda, but Widow Wallop ignored her. "Wesley — what will we do?" whimpered Wenda.

"Could be worse," whispered Wesley.

Through a wormhole in the wicker, Wenda watched. The town was now behind them, and they were wending their way through a wood, where winds were whirling and wild wolves were howling. Then they followed a winding road through a wide wetland with water lilies and yellowing willows.

They came to a wall with barbed wire on top and went through a wrought-iron gateway. Written above it was Widow Wallop's Wunderground Washery: Washes Whites Whiter than White.

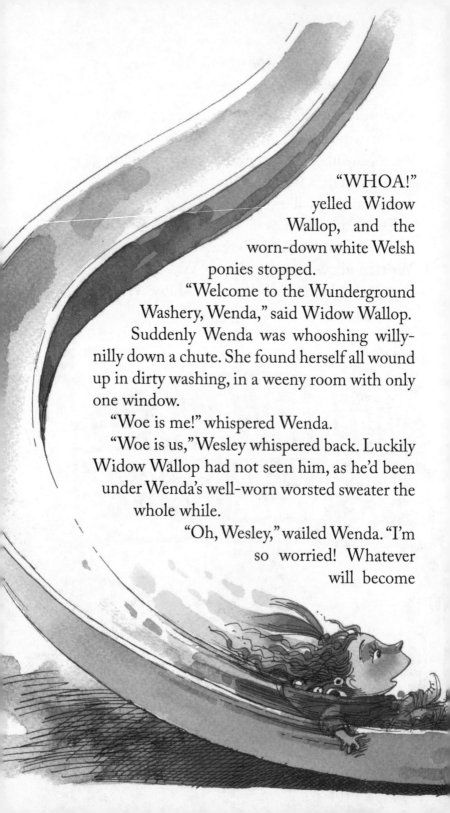

"WHOA!"
yelled Widow
Wallop, and the
worn-down white Welsh
ponies stopped.

"Welcome to the Wunderground
Washery, Wenda," said Widow Wallop.

Suddenly Wenda was whooshing willy-nilly down a chute. She found herself all wound up in dirty washing, in a weeny room with only one window.

"Woe is me!" whispered Wenda.

"Woe is us," Wesley whispered back. Luckily Widow Wallop had not seen him, as he'd been under Wenda's well-worn worsted sweater the whole while.

"Oh, Wesley," wailed Wenda. "I'm so worried! Whatever will become of us?" But Wesley was no longer awake.

Through the one window, the moon was waning, the wind was blowing the wispy clouds and the stars were twinkling in the welkin. After weeping for a while, Wenda wafted off to sleep.

Wenda awoke to a whistling of widgeons and a warbling of wrens from the woods and wetlands outside the wall with the wrought-iron gate. She felt woozy.

"Where am I?" she said.

"In Widow Wallop's Wunderground Washery," said three other voices.

What to Wenda's surprise, she and Wesley were not alone in the weeny room with the one window.

"What are your names?" she asked the three weedy, wan, waxy-faced children who were watching her.

"Wilkinson, Wu and Wanapitai," they said. "We are all waifs and strays."

Much to Wenda's wonderment, they told her that each and every one of their own wise and watchful parents had been whisked away by a weird whirlwind, just like hers, and they too

had been whooshed into the washing wagon by Widow Wallop.

"I wonder …" said Wenda.

But before she could say what she wondered, the door was wrenched open and Widow Wallop was waving her wicked-looking whip, which she wore wired to her wide waistband.

"Stop wittering, you wretched half-wits, and get to work!" she yelled.

"Wait here, Wesley," Wenda whispered to the woodchuck, covering him with her well-worn worsted sweater.

Then, in a refectory with wasps, walruses, whelks and whales on the wrinkly wallpaper, Wenda, along with Wilkinson, Wu and Wanapitai, were given wheat wafers with weevils in them, wormy whitefish, withered whortleberries and warm water that tasted of wetland water lilies.

After that they had to do weeks and weeks
of washing in the wet and weltering cellar of
the Wunderground Washery. They stood all
day at their little washtubs until their hands
were all wrinkly and their wearables were wa-
terlogged, washing, rinsing and wringing out
the whiter than white washing, and they had
to haul the wash water in weighty buckets
from the well and wrap up the clean
white washing and wedge it into
wickerwork baskets.

It was overwhelming!

"Keep working, you worms,
you wastrels!" yelled Widow Wallop, waddling in once in a while.
"Get those whites
whiter than

white! I'm warning you! I'll give you such a whack!" And she would whip their weak, weebly wrists until they had welts, while they winced and wailed. Wenda had never been so weary!

Once it was twilight, they were given more wheat wafers, then locked up in the weeny room with the dirty washing. It was whiffy in there!

"She's a weirdo," said Wilkinson. He had a whip wound on his wrist.

"Warped," said Wu. "Wow, am I ever wrecked."

"Maybe she's a werewolf," said Wanapitai, who was wheezing in a woebegone way.

"Whatever," said Wu. "Wipe your nose, would you?"

"Spare us your witticisms," said Wanapitai witheringly.

"She's wildly well-off," said Wilkinson. "She's wealthy because she doesn't worry about wages. While we're wasting away on wheat wafers with weevils and getting whooping cough from being wringing wet, she's wallowing in wiener schnitzel on Wedgewood plates, and weltering

in waffles with walnuts and whipped cream, and swilling down the wine and whiskey!"

"It's called Wunderground because you wonder if you'll ever get out," whimpered Wanapitai. "We'll never wiggle past that wall with the wire and the wrought iron, and if we did, there's the wide willowy wetland and the wild wood awash with wolves."

"Maybe she's not a widow at all — maybe she's a witch!" said Wenda.

"Could be both," said Wesley the woodchuck, coming out from under Wenda's well-worn worsted sweater. His whiskers were covered with wet sand.

"Wesley!" said Wenda. "What have you been working at all this while?"

"What are woodchucks a whiz at?" said Wesley. "Digging ways out!"

"You've widened a rabbit warren?" asked Wenda. "Wonderful!"

"Could be worse," said Wesley.

"What a worthy woodchuck! Well done!" said Wenda, Wilkinson, Wu and Wanapitai all at once.

"Woodchucks like winning," said Wesley, with a wink. "And they don't like Widow Wallop's Wunderground Washery."

Before they left, the waifs wedged the door shut with a widget of wood that Wesley had thoughtfully brought, so Widow Wallop would not know they weren't in there. Or not at first.

Then they wriggled through the workman-like widened warren Wesley had made, all the way underneath the wire-topped wall and the wrought-iron gate.

"WHOOPEE!" whispered Wanapitai, once they were outside.

"We must not waste time," said Wu.

"I wish I had wheels," said Wanapitai. "And also those two white Welsh ponies." Wanapitai had always wanted a pony.

"I wish I had wings," said Wilkinson.

"I wish I had webbed feet," said Wu.

"I wish I had weapons," said Wenda.

"Could be worse," said Wesley.

They waded through the weeds of the wide wetland, but just as they reached the willows, two things happened.

Widow Wallop in her wagon whizzed out through the wrought-iron gate of the Wunderground Washery at full gallop.

And the wild wolves came out of the woods.

"What now?" whimpered Wanapitai, wiping away a tear, as the four wide-eyed waifs cowered together. "One way or another, we'll be wasted!"

"I'll have a word with these wolves," said Wesley. "Wolves may be wild, but they respect wisdom and worship honor."

"And wolf down woodchucks," said Wu warningly.

"Not if the woodchucks know the wolf watchword," said Wesley. "I didn't spend weeks eavesdropping in widened rabbit warrens for nothing."

After Wesley had whispered in the wolves' ears, the chief wolf, who was wise but wizened, wagged his tail.

"Widow Wallop is not a wolf-friend," he said. "She does not wish us well. She has told us whoppers. We allowed her Wunderground washing wagon to wend its way through our woods in exchange for wodges of wiener schnitzel and whipped cream, but she has never given us any. And what she has been doing to these wee, weak, weedy, wandering waifs with her wicked-looking whip is just plain wrong. We declare a Wolf War!"

The Wunderground Washery wagon was almost upon them.

"Out of the way, you washed-up wolves!" yelled Widow Wallop, whipping the worn-down white Welsh ponies, who were wheezing.

"And you, wretched waifs and strays — into

the wagon at once, or I'll give you such a whack!"

All the wolves swarmed into the wagon, and there was a wrestling match, and then, Whammo! Widow Wallop was wrangled into the weeds, with a wolf gripping each wrist. But …

… she writhed out of their grasp and went wallowing back across the wetland, with the wild wolves following. First one Wellington boot was wrenched off, then the other, then the waterproof was whisked away, and then

the well-starched waistcoat. Finally, off went the wimple of wrapping paper, and there was nothing left but wooly underwear, and then …

What to Wenda's wonderment, Widow Wallop was not a widow at all! Widow Wallop was not even a woman! Widow Wallop was a man! Which explained the wiry eyebrows.

"Well, well," said the chief wolf, who had read the WANTED poster. "The missing Wizard Willup, the Whirlwind Whiz, hiding out as a Washerwoman! One-trick Willup — whirlwinds were all he could ever work up! Wasted our woods once with a whirlwind, the weasel!"

"I'm good at whist, too," whined the wizard.

"Not good enough," said the chief wolf. "Watch that whip of his, it's really a wand. Now, instead of that wiener schnitzel you never gave us, we have you!

And he licked his whiskers.

"Wait!" wheedled Wizard Willup. "One more wager! This can be a win-win! You can wolf down these weeny weaklings and that wretched woodchuck, plus all the wiener schnitzels you want! And I'll throw in some whelks, and walruses, and wrapping paper, and ..."

"Or we can wolf down YOU," said the chief wolf. "What do you wish?" he asked the four children. "We await your word."

"All we want is our wise and watchful parents, who were whisked away by this wizard in weird whirlwinds," said Wenda. "So he could turn us into waifs and strays, and work us in the washery until we wilted."

"And we want no more whipping," said Wu.

"And we want no more washing," said Wilkinson.

"And the worn-down white Welsh ponies must be set free," said Wanapitai.

"Well?" said the chief wolf to Wizard Willup. "Is it rewind those whirlwinds, or wolf stew?"

The wizard knew when he was walloped. Whining in a wavering way, he waved the whip that was really a wand, and, whirling and swirling …

…out of the wispy clouds came the four sets of wise and watchful parents.

"Wenda! Wu! Wilkinson! Wanapitai!" they whooped.

"WHEE! WOWIE! ZOWIE!"

"Wesley, you've been wonderful," said Wenda, hugging the worthy, wuzzy woodchuck. The Welsh ponies whickered, and the wolves wagged their tails.

"All's well that ends well," said the chief wolf.

"Could be worse," said Wesley.

"Now, let us all wend our way homeward," said the wise and watchful mothers, "and have some waffles with walnuts and whipped cream."

"And maybe a wee drop of whiskey," whispered the fathers.

The wolves were awarded the whopping reward and bought wads and wads of wieners with it.

The white Welsh ponies went to live with Wanapitai.

Wesley the woodchuck visits Wandering Wenda every Wednesday. She waits for him at the window, and her mother has woven him his very own well-worn worsted sweater.

As for Wizard Willup, the wild wolves weighted down his wicked wand and sank it in the waves and water lilies of the willowy wetland, and whisked him back to Widow Wallop's Wunderground Washery ...

... where he had a lot of well water to haul, and weeks and weeks and weeks of whiter than white washing work to do.

MARGARET ATWOOD is the author of more than forty books of fiction, poetry and critical essays. Her most recent books include *Hag-Seed*, a novel revisitation of Shakespeare's play *The Tempest*, and *Angel Catbird* — featuring a cat-bird superhero — a graphic novel with co-creator Johnnie Christmas. She is a two-time winner of the Governor General's Literary Award, has won the Man Booker Prize and was inducted into Canada's Walk of Fame. Margaret Atwood lives in Toronto with writer Graeme Gibson.

DUŠAN PETRIČIĆ is the award-winning illustrator of more than twenty books for children. Most recently, he has illustrated *Snap!* by Hazel Hutchins, *InvisiBill* by Maureen Fergus and *My Family Tree and Me*, which he also wrote. A former professor of illustration and book design, Petričić's work appeared for years in the *New York Times*, *Scientific American*, the *Wall Street Journal* and the *Toronto Star*. He continues to work as a political cartoonist for *Politika* and to illustrate for other magazines. He lives in Belgrade and Toronto.